THE ADVENTURES OF SANDI & CLAMMY

BY DORA HENDERSON
LMHC, Registered Play Therapist

COLORING SHEETS BASED ON ILLUSTRATIONS BY DONNA COFFEE AND HEATHER WORLEY

Many thanks to Darryl, Nathan,
Brandon & Caitlynn Henderson
for being an awesome family.

THE ADVENTURES OF SANDI & CLAMMY

Sandi and the Tides of Change

Sandi was a grumpy grain of sand living in a reef.

Every day, she would watch fish and other
animals swim and play around her.

"If only I had spines or spikes,
a shell or fins!" she groaned.
"Then I would not be stuck on the
ocean floor, alone and ugly!"

Clammy was a wise old clam living in the same reef as Sandi. Clammy was nothing like the grumpy grain of sand. She was always singing and encouraging others. Clammy was thoughtful and quick to perform a good deed whenever anyone was in need.

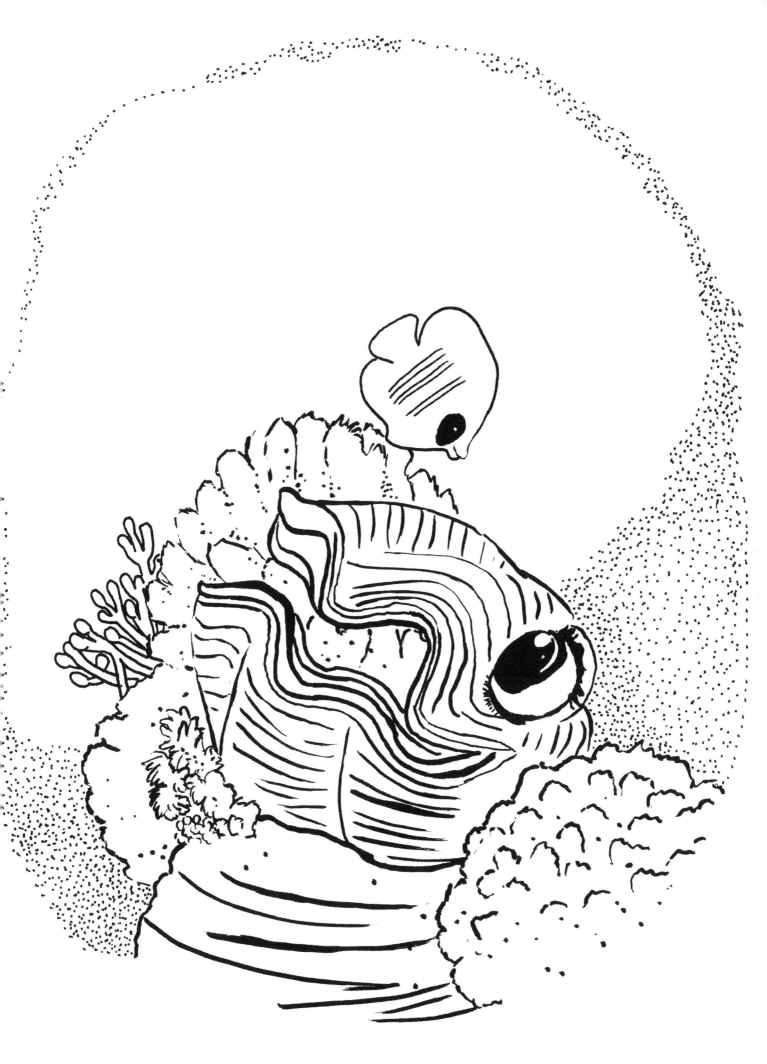

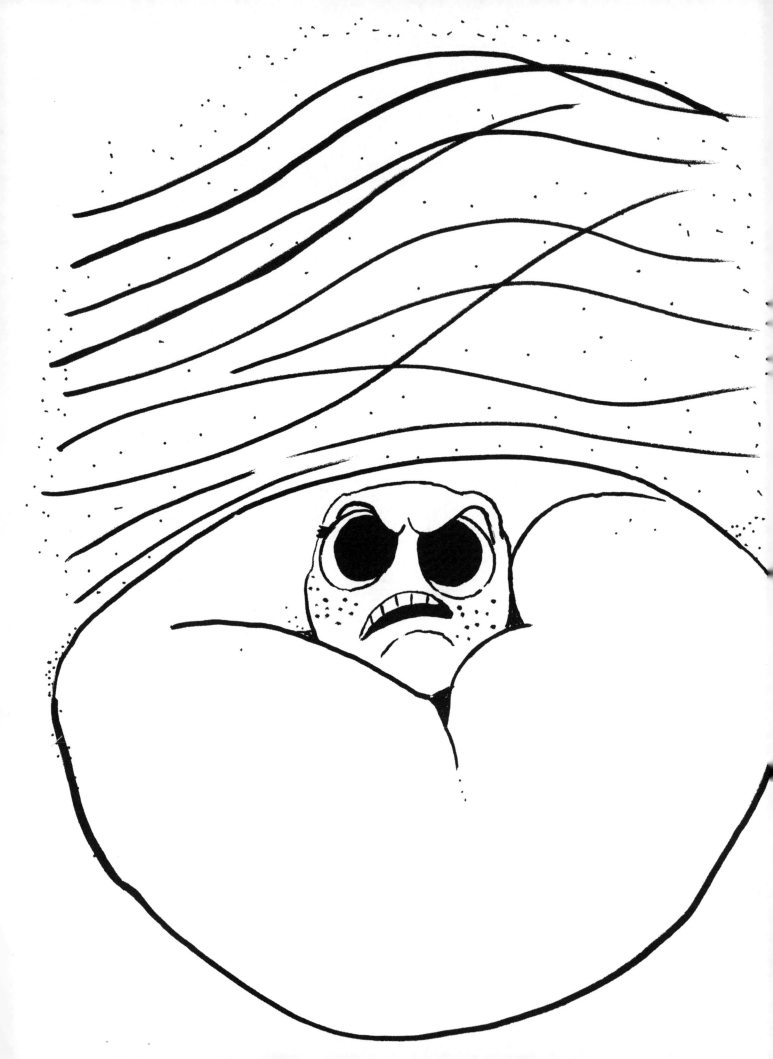

One day, a big storm hit the reef and caught
Sandi by surprise; before she knew it, she was
being carried away by the tide! Sandi was tossed
and thrown until she landed in some strange goo.

"Now what's happened?
Where have I landed?" she huffed.
"I am worse off now than I was before."

"Hello!" said a voice from above Sandi.
"My name is Clammy. Welcome to my home!"
The storm had carried Sandi all the way
into Clammy's shell, and now the friendly mollusc
was introducing herself.

"Close your shell!" barked Sandi.
"I am far from home and want to be alone!"
Even though Sandi was rude, Clammy became
quiet and settled in with her new guest.

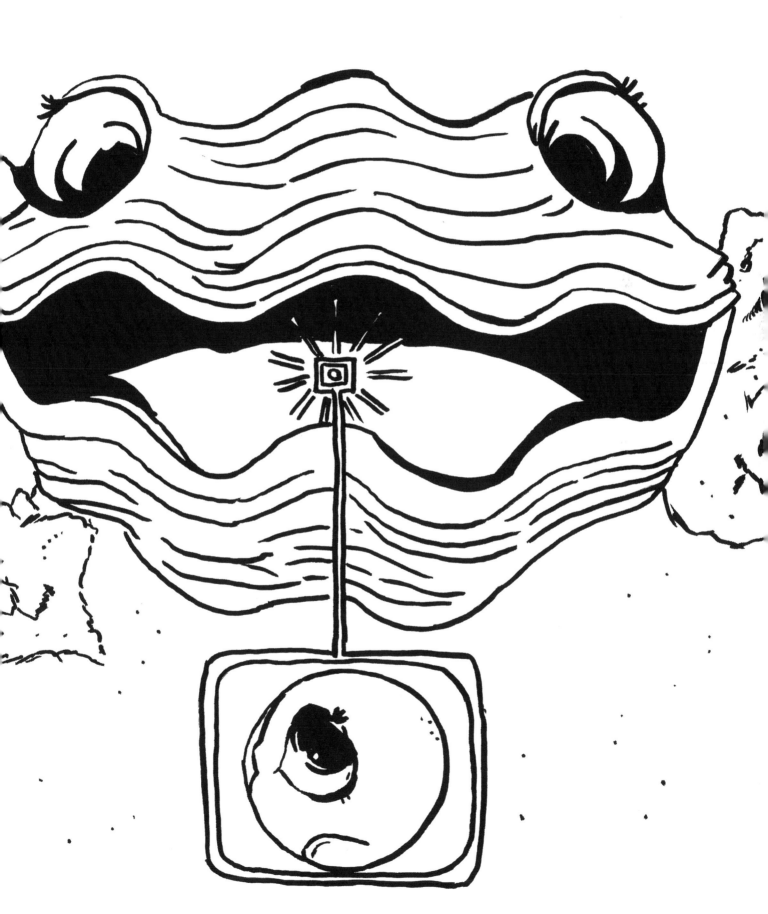

Each day was a challenge, but Clammy continued
to be nice to her new roommate. Sandi, on the
other hand, continued to be a grump. Sandi complained
day after day, telling Clammy she could never be as
great as those that could swim or had fins.
But Clammy never stopped being nice; she told
Sandi she was as special as a gem.

Sandi did not believe she was special at all!
"I live at the bottom of our reef! How am I unique?"

But Clammy knew just what to say.
"If you start to think you are special, you will soon
believe it! You will be surprised at what you could become."

Sandi thought about what Clammy said.
Maybe she was right. Clammy had been
so nice to her, so it was worth a try.

Sandi began to feel better the more she used kind words and thoughts. Soon her grumpiness faded away. "Changing the way I think makes me feel good! Thank you for being so nice to me, Clammy!"

Sandi had changed and believed she was as special as a gem. Not only that, but she looked on the outside how she felt on the inside, all thanks to her new friend, Clammy. "Thank you for all your have done," she said to Clammy. "I think from now on, I would like to be called Pearly!" From that day, Clammy and Pearly were the best of friends at the bottom of the reef.

Sandi struggled with negative thoughts that were tearing her down and making her feel sad, and unhappy inside. Thoughts can either build you up or tear you down. Clammy helped Sandi learn to build up her self-esteem by using positive self-talk. Here are some examples you can try: "I am unique and different from everyone else", "I am ok just as I am", "I am awesome."

Write down a list of positive statements you can use to build you up and make you strong.

_____

Everyone is unique and special. Sandi discovered that she was a very beautiful treasure both inside and out.

Draw or write about your special and unique qualities.

_____

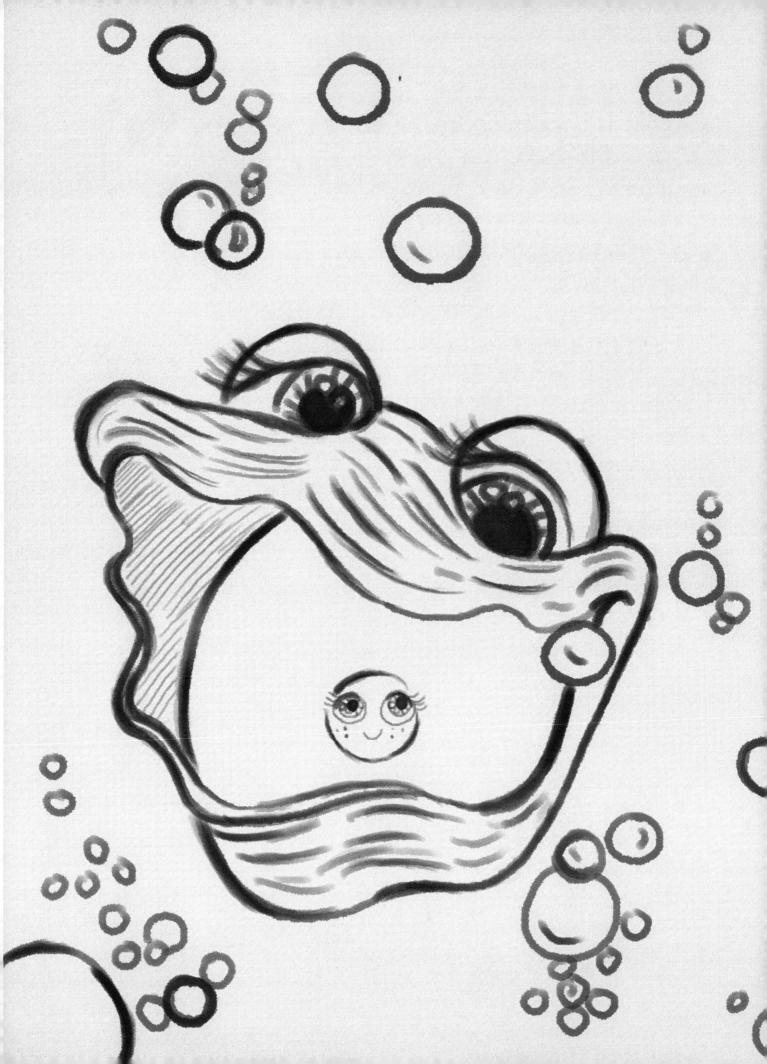

Clammy
Opens Up

Down in the warm sand at the bottom of a reef,
there was once a clam and her pearl who were best friends.
Pearly had once been a grain of sand named Sandi.
Pearly grew bigger and more beautiful day by day as a
brilliant pearl, because her friend, Clammy, was kind.

The two friends had fun every day,
sharing their happiness with their reef
neighbors and friends, and spreading kindness
to anyone they met. Pearly and Clammy knew
their friendship would last forever.

Even though they believed they would never be apart, Clammy had a terrible dream one night that Pearly was taken away because of how big and beautiful she turned out to be. This worried Clammy, but Pearly was calm. She told Clammy that it was just a dream, that's all.

One bright morning at the bottom of the reef,
Clammy and Pearly were singing a song together
as they did every day. Clammy's mouth was wide open
as she belted out their favorite tunes. They sang
with their whole hearts, the melody spreading over
the reef until Clammy suddenly did not hear
Pearly singing any more.

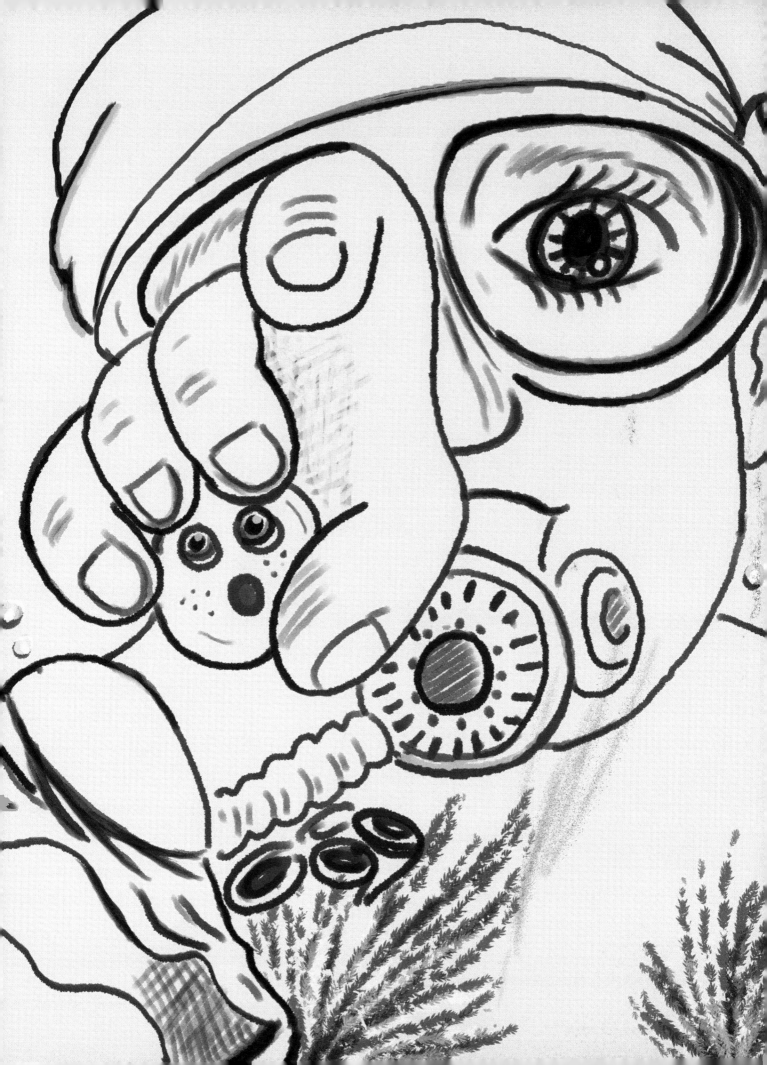

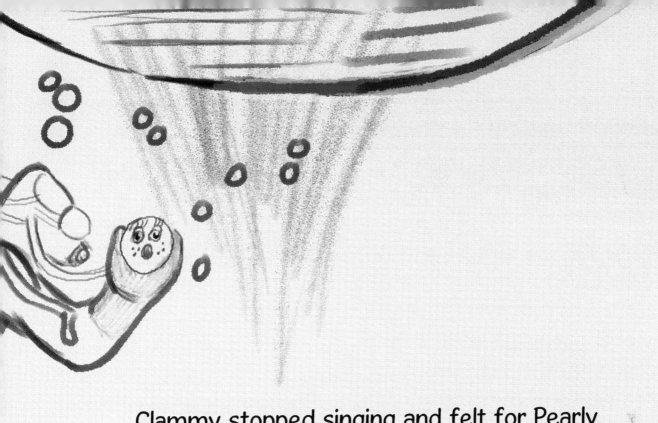

Clammy stopped singing and felt for Pearly
on her tongue, feeling shocked and scared when
she could not find her friend there. Then she saw
a diver carrying Pearly away, and Clammy never
saw her best friend again after that day.

Her only best friend was gone. The old clam
at the bottom of the reef never felt so
heartbroken and sad in her whole life. All she could
do now was cry and wish Pearly was back.
Clammy locked her shell up tight and felt very alone.

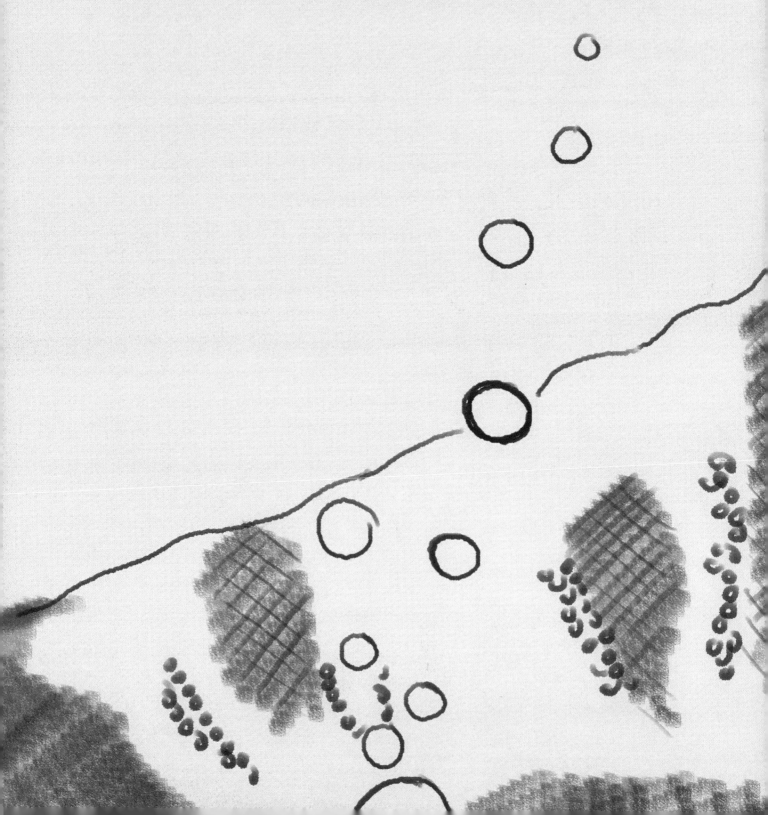

Clammy stayed in the sand and was quiet
for many days after Pearly was taken, something
strange for such a friendly mollusc. She had spent
so much time caring for others, but now she felt
no one would care for her.

The friends Clammy had been so nice
to saw how upset she was now and
decided to help her, as she had helped
them so many times before.

All the clams came together
to talk to her about all the pearls
they lost too, and Clammy did not
feel so alone anymore.

Clammy was thankful for her friends
who had given her hope. They told Clammy
that everyone has friends that come and go,
but remembering the special times we had
with them is what will stay with us forever.

Coping skills are tools that can help you feel better
when you feel sad, lonely, or hurt. The following are a few
ideas you can try: reading, painting, listening to music,
drawing in a journal, or even taking slow deep breaths.
Can you think of any other ideas to help you feel better?
Draw or write them down.

_____

Clammy lost her friend, Pearly, and felt very sad and lonely. Remember, it is ok to have these feelings. They are normal. Draw a picture or write about a time you may have felt sad or lonely. (Don't forget to use your coping skills).

_____

Clammy learned that it was ok to feel sad and to cry. Clammy learned that she needed to use her coping skills and shared her feelings with her friends.

Draw a picture of people that you feel safe to talk to.

_____

Imagine Clammy is your friend.
What would you say to encourage her?

_____

Dora Henderson is a licensed mental health counselor
who also earned an added certificate as a play therapist.
Dora has added trainings in sand tray therapy as well
as with EMDR. Dora is a mother of 3 children and has been
married for 29 years. Dora is a mental health counselor for
a local school district in Orlando, Florida, and has a passion for
working with children as well as adults. Sandi and Clammy
came out of the desire to make sure that all children learn
some basic CBT (Cognitive Behavioral Therapy) to assist
children in gaining the ability to increase their positive
self-talk skills, thus increasing self-regulation skills
and positive self esteem.

Made in the USA
Columbia, SC
31 July 2021